Tips for Reading Together

Children learn best when reading is fun.

- Talk about the title and the pictures on the cover.
- Look through the pictures together and discuss what you think the story might be about.
- Read the story together, pointing to the words and inviting your child to join in.
- Give lots of praise as your child reads with you, and help them when necessary.
- Have fun finding the hidden butterflies.
- Enjoy re-reading the story and encourage your child to say the repeated phrases with you.

Children enjoy reading stories again and again.
This helps to build their confidence.

Have fun!

Find the butterfly hidden in every picture.

Floppy and
the Bone

Cynthia Rider • Alex Brychta

OXFORD

UNIVERSITY PRESS

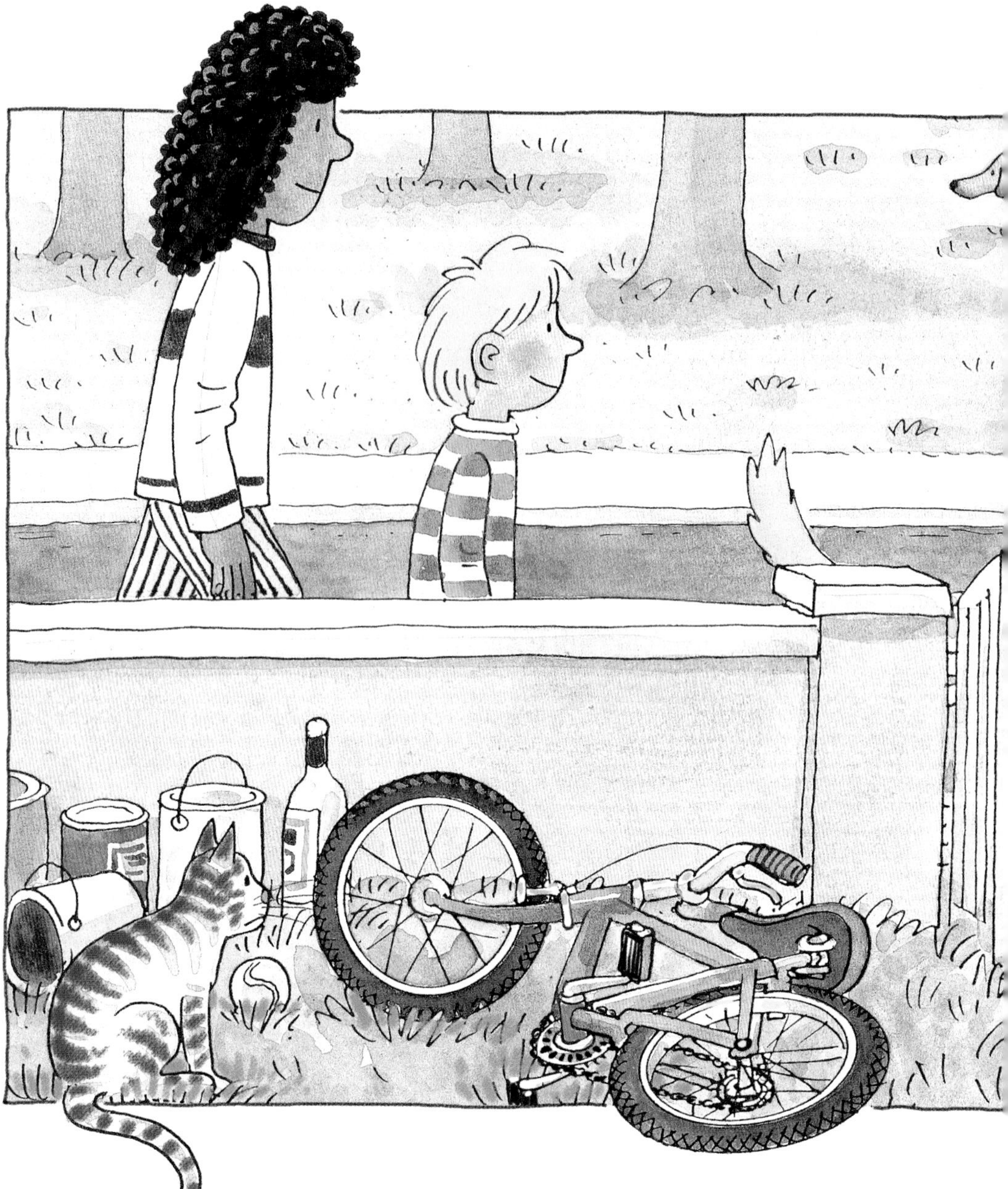

Floppy saw a big bone.

"I want that bone,"
said Floppy.

So he took it!

"Stop! Stop!" said Biff.

"Drop the bone!" said Chip.

But Floppy didn't stop,
and he didn't drop the bone!

He ran up the hill.

He ran into a wood...

and onto a bridge...
and stopped!

Floppy looked down.

He saw a dog in the water.

The dog had a big bone.

Floppy wanted that bone, too.

Grrrrrrrrr!
went Floppy.

SPLASH! went the bone.
SPLASH! went Floppy.

"Oh no!" said Floppy.
"The dog I saw was me!"

Think about the story

Why do you think Floppy took the bone?

What did Floppy see in the water? Did he think it was a real dog?

Do you think Floppy was a sensible dog in this story?

Have you ever wanted something as much as Floppy wanted his bone?

Picture puzzle

How many things can you find beginning with the same sound as the 'b' in **b**all?

> **Useful common words repeated in this story and other books at Level 2.**
>
> big   dog   he   stop   that   the   went
>
> Names in this story: Biff   Chip   Floppy

(Answer to picture puzzle: ball, bike, bottle, bowl, boy, bush, butterfly)

More books for you to enjoy

Level 1:
Getting Ready

Level 2:
Starting to Read

Level 3:
Becoming a Reader

Level 4:
Building Confidence

OXFORD
UNIVERSITY PRESS

Great Clarendon Street,
Oxford OX2 6DP

Text © Cynthia Rider –
adapted by the author from
an Aesop fable 2005
Illustrations © Alex Brychta 2005
Designed by Andy Wilson

First published 2005

British Library Cataloguing
in Publication Data available

ISBN 0 19 838559 5

10 9 8 7 6 5 4 3 2 1

Printed in China by Imago